THE TALKING POT

❧ A Danish Folktale ❧

Retold by Virginia Haviland

Illustrated by Melissa Sweet

Little, Brown and Company   Boston Toronto London

First Edition

This story originally appeared in *Favorite Fairy Tales Told
in Denmark* (Little, Brown, 1971) by Virginia Haviland,
who retold the folktale with some adaptation from *Danish
Fairy and Folk Tales, A Collection of Popular Stories and
Fairy Tales*, translated by J. Christian Bay from the Danish
of Svend Grundtwid, E. T. Kristensen, Ingvor Bondeesen,
and L. Budde. New York and London, Harper, 1899.

Library of Congress Cataloging-in-Publication Data

Haviland, Virginia, 1911–
    The talking pot : a Danish folktale / retold by Virginia
Haviland; illustrated by Melissa Sweet. — 1st ed.
        p.   cm.
    Summary: A retelling of a Danish tale in which a magical
talking pot causes a poor family to triumph over a rich couple.
    ISBN 0-316-35060-5
    [1. Folklore — Denmark.]   I. Sweet, Melissa, ill.   II. Title.
PZ8.1.H315Tal   1990
398.21'09489 — dc20
[E]   89-24722
                                                                                  CIP
                                                                                   AC

10 9 8 7 6 5 4 3 2 1

Joy Street Books are published by
Little, Brown and Company (Inc.)

WOR

Published simultaneously in Canada
by Little, Brown & Company (Canada) Limited

Printed in the United States of America

To Joan and Spellman,
with gratitude

M.S.

A man and his wife were once living in a very small cottage — the smallest and poorest hut in the whole village. They were so poor that they often lacked even their daily bread. They had been obliged to sell nearly everything they had, but had managed somehow to keep their only cow. At length they decided that the cow, too, must go, and the man led her away, intending to take her to market.

As he walked along the road a stranger hailed him, asking if he intended to sell the animal, and how much he would take for it.

"I think," answered he, "that a hundred crowns would be a fair price."

"Money I cannot give you," said the stranger, "but I have something which is worth as much as a hundred crowns. Here is a pot which I am willing to exchange for your cow." And he showed the man an iron pot with three legs and a handle.

"A pot!" exclaimed the cow's owner. "What possible use would that be to me when I have nothing to put in it? My wife and children cannot eat an iron pot. No, money is what I need and what I must have."

hile the two men looked at each other and at the cow and the pot, the three-legged thing suddenly began to speak. "Just take me," it said. The poor man thought that if the pot could speak, no doubt it could do more than that. So he closed the bargain, took the pot, and returned home with it.

When he reached his hut he went first to the stall where the cow had been tied, for he was afraid to appear before his wife at once. He tied the pot to the manger, went into the hut, and asked for something to eat. He was hungry from his long walk.

"Well," said his wife, "did you make a good bargain at the market? Did you get a good price for the cow?"

"Yes," he said, "the price was fair enough."

"That is well," she returned. "The money will help us a long time."

"No," he sighed, "I received no money for the cow."

"Dear me!" she cried. "What did you receive, then?" He told her to go and look in the cow's stall.

As soon as the woman learned that the three-legged pot was all that had been paid him for the cow, she scolded and abused her husband. "You are a great blockhead!" she cried. "I wish I myself had taken the cow to market! I never heard of such foolishness!" Thus she went on and on.

But, "Clean me and put me on the fire," suddenly shouted the pot.

The woman opened her eyes in wonder, and now it was her turn to think that if the pot could talk, no doubt it could do more than this. She cleaned and washed it carefully and put it on the fire.

I skip, I skip!" cried the pot.

"How far do you skip?" asked the woman.

"To the rich man's house, to the rich man's house!" it answered, running from the fireplace to the door, across the yard, and up the road, as fast as its three short legs would carry it.

he rich man, who had never shared anything with the poor, lived not very far away. His wife was baking bread when the pot came running in and jumped up on the table. "Ah," exclaimed the woman, "isn't this wonderful! I need you for a pudding that must be baked at once." Thereupon she began to heap good things into the pot—flour, sugar, butter, raisins, almonds,

spices, and so on. And the pot received it all with a good will. At length the pudding was made, but when the rich man's wife reached for it, intending to put it on the stove, tap, tap, tap went the three short legs, and the pot stood on the threshold of the open door. "Dear me, where are you going with my pudding?" cried the woman. "To the poor man's home," replied the pot, running down the road at a great speed.

When the poor couple saw the pot skipping back to them, with the pudding in it, they rejoiced. The man lost no time in asking his wife whether the bargain did not seem to be an excellent one, after all.

"Yes," she agreed. She was pleased and contented.

ext morning the pot cried again, "I skip, I skip!"

"How far do you skip?" they asked.

"To the rich man's barn!" it shouted, running up the road. When it arrived at the barn it hopped through the doorway. "Look at that black pot!" cried the men, who were threshing wheat. "Let us see how much it will hold." They poured a bushel of wheat into it, but it did not seem to fill. Another bushel went in, but there was still more room. When every grain of wheat had been given to the pot, it seemed capable of holding still more.

ut as there was no more wheat to be found, the three short legs began to move, and when the men looked around, the pot had reached the gate.

"Stop, stop!" they called. "Where do you go with our wheat?"

"To the poor man's home," replied the pot, speeding down the road and leaving the men behind, dismayed and dumbfounded.

The poor people were delighted. The wheat they received was enough to feed them for several years.

On the third morning, the pot again skipped up the road. It was a beautiful day. The sun shone so brightly that the rich man had spread his money on a table near his open window to allow the sunshine to clear the mold from his gold. All at once the pot stood on the table before him. He was counting his coins, as wealthy men like to do, and although he could not imagine where this black pot

had come from, he thought it would make a fine place to store his money. So he threw in one handful of coins after another, until the pot held them all. At that very moment the pot jumped from the table to the windowsill.

"Wait!" shouted the man. "Where do you go with all my money?"

"To the poor man's home," returned the pot, skipping down the road with the money dancing within it.

n the center of the poor man's hut it stopped, and when its owners saw the unexpected treasure, they cried out in rapture.

"Clean and wash me," said the pot, "and put me aside."

Next morning the pot announced again that it was ready to skip.

"How far do you skip?" asked the man and his wife.

"To the rich man's house!" So it ran up the road again, never stopping until it had reached the rich man's kitchen.

he man happened to be there himself this time, and as soon as he saw the pot he cried, "There is that pot that carried away our pudding, our wheat, and all our money! I shall make it return what it stole!"

The man flung himself upon the pot, but found that he was unable to get off again.

"I skip, I skip!" shouted the pot.

"Skip to the North Pole, if you wish!" yelled the man, furiously trying to free himself. But the three short legs moved on, carrying him rapidly down the road.

he poor man and his wife saw it pass their door, but it never thought of stopping. For all that I know, it went straight on, carrying its burden to the North Pole.

The poor couple were now rich. They thought often of the wonderful pot with the three short legs that skipped so cheerfully for their good. But it was gone, and they have never seen it since.

Baked Danish Apple Pudding

½ cup all-purpose flour

½ cup light brown sugar,
    packed in cup

1 teaspoon ground cinnamon

1 teaspoon baking powder

¼ teaspoon nutmeg

¼ teaspoon salt

½ cup raisins

½ cup slivered or
    chopped almonds

2 tablespoons very soft or
    melted butter

1 egg, lightly beaten

1 cup (2 small) tart apples,
    pared, cored, and chopped

This recipe doesn't have to be baked in a talking pot. A common cake pan will do nicely! Here's how:

Preheat oven to 350°F. Butter an 8-inch round cake pan or 1 quart-sized, shallow ovenproof round casserole.

Measure all of the ingredients into a large mixing bowl. With a wooden spoon stir until well mixed and all dry ingredients are moist. (Mixture will seem very dry at first, but as you stir, it will become moist.)

Turn into the prepared pan and spread until smooth. Bake for 25 to 30 minutes or until a toothpick inserted in the center comes out clean. Serve warm, cut in wedges, with whipped cream or ice cream on top. Makes about 6 servings.

We are grateful to Beatrice Ojakangas, author of *The Great Scandinavian Baking Book* (Little, Brown, 1988), for providing us with the recipe for Baked Danish Apple Pudding.